CW00859937

ALSO BY E. C. HIBBS

RUN LIKE CLOCKWORK
Vol I: The Ruby Rings
Vol II: The Eternal Heart

THE FOXFIRES TRILOGY
The Winter Spirits
The Mist Children
The Night River

THE TRAGIC SILENCE SERIES
Sepia and Silver
The Libelle Papers
Tragic Silence
Darkest Dreams

Blindsighted Wanderer
The Sailorman's Daughters
Night Journeys: Anthology
The Hollow Hills Tarot Deck

Blood and Scales (anthology co-author)
Dare to Shine (anthology co-author)
Fae Thee Well (anthology co-author)

AS CHARLOTTE E. BURGESS
Into the Woods and Far Away: A Collection of Faery Meditations
Gentle Steps: Meditations for Anxiety and Depression

The Sailorman's Daughters

E. C. Hibbs

For Faith,

Hear the song of the sea...

For Rhian,

Amazing friend and mermaid at heart.

Chapter  One

Cornwall, 1837

The view of the sea from the Lover's Leap was breath-taking enough, but Connie always felt it pull at her heart the most when dusk set in. As the summer sky shot with pink and gold, she would scramble up the steep incline above the village of Trewhella, and seat herself on the peak, letting time draw out around her. It was something she'd done many times, even though getting caught would mean a good scolding from her mother.

Connie gazed across the water, letting her eyes blur with the tumbling waves. Great headlands rose around her, protruding their sheer faces into a beautiful abyss. The wind was gentle, and she could see the sinking sun reflected almost perfectly near the horizon. The vessels in the harbour creaked and groaned as men secured the rigging; brought in the day's catches. The unmistakable coastal smells of fish and salt wafted up Connie's nose.

It was stunning. Sometimes she found a small part of herself shocked to think of what happened here, when the *Senara* mysteriously sunk far out to sea. She could barely imagine the mourning shrieks of the poor widows whose husbands had been taken by the great wreck; the way the sea boiled red in the little cove when they threw themselves from the cliff. Ever since that fateful day, it had been said in Trewhella that the winds had changed, and now howled around the rocks with the tormented souls of the lost.

Connie wasn't sure whether she believed them. The tragedy happened when she was a babe in arms, and she had no memory of what life had been like before it. She just knew that besides the endless fishing, things had become far from normal. Now, eleven years later, she was the daughter of the one sailor who had come back home.

The sun set; and Connie quickly grabbed her basket before running down to the village, brushing the grass off her skirts as she went.

*

The place was a hubbub of noise and movement as the nets were hauled out. Fish flapped clumsily on the quay amid thick coils of salt-hardened rope. As they were loaded onto wagons and the boats given their final checks, Connie slipped carefully down the backstreets, until she arrived at a rickety house near the flats. Waves smacked against the rocks below and sprayed her with foam as she slipped through the door.

The mouth-watering smell of vegetable pie wafted from the open stove, accompanied by the bubbling kettle filled with sweet tea. Her mother, Dawn, was rolling a skein of wool in her hands. As soon as the latch clicked, she looked up at Connie with eyes made permanently dark from fatigue.

"You are late," she remarked.

Connie placed the basket on the table and Dawn peered inside. It was filled with wild berries and herbs from the back fields, which Connie had been gathering all afternoon.

"I had to get past the sailormen," Connie insisted. She smoothed her apron as carefully as she could, in case any stray blades of grass were still clinging to it.

Dawn emptied the basket and set about tying the herbs into bundles. As she hung them from the rafters to dry, Connie glanced across the room to where her father was sitting. Like always, he was at the window, not moving, with the same bland listlessness in his bloodshot eyes. His face was flushed from years of living off gin, and his belly had swelled until he seemed moulded into his chair. He let out a loud snorting sigh, gaze never leaving the water.

Dawn wiped at her forehead with a handkerchief; then took the kettle off the hook to pour a flask of tea. Without needing to be told, Connie grasped it and moved towards the back of the house. Sitting in the corner in a creaky rocking chair, was a tiny old lady named Granny Florence. She wasn't actually related to the family in any way, but Dawn had taken her in when the fish stocks ran low and never had the heart to send her away later. No-one else in the village would have kept her; she had a penchant for ranting and raving like a madwoman. There was a rumour that she was almost a hundred years old already, and would never die to make life easier for everyone.

The typical cocktail of nervousness and fascination mixed within Connie as she handed over the flask. Florence wrapped her gnarled fingers around it and took a shaky sip.

"Would you like anything else, Granny?" Connie asked, clasping her hands together meekly.

Florence glanced at her with a pair of squinting eyes. "It's too hot... too hot!" she shrieked, slamming the flask on the table. Some of the contents splashed out and Connie ran to get a cloth.

"I want food," said Florence.

"The pie is nearly ready," Connie assured.

"Not pie!" Florence snapped. "I want fillet!"

Connie shook her head. "We can have fillet tomorrow, now the catch has been brought in."

Florence quietened, looking at her intently. Connie gave a soft smile and went to go back to her mother, when Florence's hand shot out and snatched her wrist.

"You've been doing something you shouldn't."

Connie's heart hammered. "No, I haven't."

"You can't lie to me, lass." Florence let go and wryly tapped the side of her nose with one finger. "The Leap?"

Connie stammered. "I never... I haven't done anything –"

"Calm down, girl. I'm no telltale. Now answer me. I know you go up there."

Connie bit her lip. It was more unnerving to see these moments of intelligent clarity in Florence than if she was completely demented. It was so hard to predict her when she was in a mood like this, able to change from one moment to the next. But when she wanted to be, she was as sharp as nails, and Connie knew there was no way around it.

She glanced over her shoulder to be sure Dawn wouldn't hear. "Yes."

Florence smirked to herself. "Not surprising, really. Have you ever been into the cove?"

"No."

"Probably a good thing. The mermaids would have you if you did."

Connie quickly held back an exasperated sigh.

"You don't believe me?" Florence hissed. "Why else do you think the widows leapt to their deaths? The mermaids took their husbands and then sent the song to their loves on land! The lament of the ocean is why they threw themselves into the black beyond!"

"Hush now," Dawn called, too used to the mermaid-rant. "The pie is ready!"

"I want fillet!" shouted Florence. Then her eyes stopped rolling and looked at Connie again. "I dare you, lass!" she whispered. "I dare you to go to the cove, and see if you can hear the singing!"

*

That night, Connie woke to the sound of her parents arguing. She sat up in bed, clutching her moth-eaten teddy to her chest. The resonance of angered voices, albeit hushed, was as strange as it was horrid. Despite herself, Connie listened, trying to make out the words.

"I'm almost at the end of my tether!" her mother was snarling. "It's hard enough trying to provide for the four of us without you drinking all my money away!"

"Then get a job that pays better than washing clothes, woman. All that scented water makes the place stink."

"There are no other jobs, Albert, better or otherwise! It would be a great help if you got up and did something to help me! Or is a notion like that beyond occurring to you?"

"You will not speak to me that way, Dawn Marner! I am your husband!"

"And a fat lot of good you are at it! You do nothing! You ignore me and you ignore your daughter! We might as well be part of the walls for the amount of attention you pay us!"

Connie closed her eyes despondently. It was true. Albert had never really been a father to her; and because of it, her mother's mind had been stretched to the limit as well. Part of her hated him for it. He'd not only denied them love; his reputation as the lone survivor of the *Senara* had meant she'd grown up with no friends. None of the orphans left from the disaster wanted to know *her*, with both parents still living.

"I wish for the spray of the sea in my face again," Albert said. "You will deny me that."

"I deny you nothing! Don't I give you everything? Haven't I always? And how have you repaid me other than with strife? Connie is the only good thing to have come of us, and God knows she deserves better than you."

"I don't want her."

Connie's heart froze. The silence surrounded her as she grasped at her teddy. Had she honestly just heard him say that?

"You cannot be serious!" Dawn cried.

"I don't want you either." Her father's words were slow, deliberate. "You're my wife and she's my daughter. And I tolerate you all under my roof because I'm bound to. I married you before I went away to sea, and I was a fool. You are not my Raniira, Dawn. You give nothing worthy of me. And neither does the girl."

Horrified, Connie fell against the wall. Her hands trembled and she stared into the darkness of the room. She felt tears creeping up on her; quickly held them at bay. She was alone, but didn't want to give Albert the satisfaction of her hurt.

She stayed awake for what seemed like hours. Gradually her parents' voices died away, and the house became quiet. Chest tight from holding in her sobs, Connie threw back her blankets and pulled a thin shawl over her nightgown before slipping out of the window.

The cool summer night swelled around her. She didn't need a lantern; the moon was full and bright, sending a ghostly glow over the waves. Desperate to get away, if only for a little while, she ran through the abandoned streets towards the Lover's Leap. Its huge face leered against the sky, like an arm curling around Trewhella, and seemed even higher in the lack of sunlight.

She meant to run up it again to her spot at the peak, but then she remembered Florence's words and stilled. Her eyes moved to the base of the Leap, where a group of tall tooth-like rocks concealed the cove.

And then she heard it. As the wind blew, it didn't carry the moans of grieving souls. Tonight, it sounded like the songs of whales. But there was a clearness and clarity which even the magnificent animals couldn't hold, as though the music was being channelled through a glass bell.

Her anger ebbed away as she listened. Entranced, she wandered down onto the flats. The wet muddy sand welled between her bare toes. She grabbed at her hair to stop it flapping around her face; then carefully ducked between the rocks. They were slippery with seaweed, and barnacles dug their hard shells into her feet, but she found a handhold and used it to keep herself above the worst of the pools.

She couldn't hold back a gasp of wonder.

Sitting on a flat black slab just out of the sea was a beautiful woman. Her skin was pale and shimmered like a pearl, decorated with sashes of seaweed. Wavy tresses of golden hair flowed down her back and over her shoulder, and she ran her fingers through it gently as she combed out knots.

But what struck Connie the most was the long silvery tail that curled around the bottom of the slab. The fins at its base arched like that of a whale; smaller ones flickered at her hips. And out of her mouth, the song was flowing, in a voice more powerful and haunting than any human could ever manage.

Connie couldn't bring herself to look away. She barely even blinked, wanting to imprint this being in her mind forever. Florence hadn't been lying or spouting nonsense after all! There were mermaids! Right here, barely half a mile outside Trewhella!

The woman's final note died away as the wind silenced. Then it picked up again, but a different voice began the melody: younger, less experienced. Connie looked around for it, and was even more startled to find another mermaid, just a few feet away. The position of the rocks had kept her concealed before, but now Connie could see her clearly as she moved with the song.

The other mermaid looked around Connie's age, or perhaps a little younger. Like the older one – who Connie supposed was her mother – her hair was a lustrous blonde, and an orange starfish clung to the left side of her scalp. She swept her tail back and forth in rhythm with the music.

Suddenly, Connie's grip slipped and she fell into the rock pool with a splash. Both the mermaids stiffened, dark eyes wide.

"Come, Heloise!" the older one called, diving forwards. The young mermaid threw herself down onto the sand and began wriggling towards the surf on her belly.

Connie darted into the open, hands in the air. "Wait, please! I won't hurt you!"

But the young mermaid didn't listen. Connie had barely taken a single step after her before she too disappeared under the surface. And then Connie was alone once again, staring into the distance as water lapped around her ankles.

Chapter  Two

The next day, Connie walked with her mother and Florence to join the villagers in the church. Dawn had been too busy to take much notice of her damp nightgown, so Connie hung it on the clothes line, letting it dry with the rest of the laundry. Then she'd joined her family by the hearth, all of them dressed in black – all except for Albert, who remained in his chair.

Nothing had been said of the argument. But Connie could tell from the way her mother was holding herself that she was broken inside, and she whispered through tight lips; a light gone from her eyes. Like Connie, the truth was something Dawn had known for a while, but hearing it, with such certainty, was a hammer-strike. And, in typical fashion, Albert barely batted an eyelid at the prospect of what he'd done.

As she settled in the pew, Connie remembered the carefully guarded look of disgust she'd given her father when they left the house. More than ever, his lack of acknowledgement stung like a wasp had somehow gotten inside her chest. Who was Raniira? What had happened to make him wish his own family away?

Her eyes were drawn to an old carving set into the wall near the altar. It had been there for decades, and showed a creature with the torso of a woman and tail of a dolphin.

The vicar walked down the aisle and led them all in prayer. Connie bowed her head obediently and sent her thoughts to the souls of the drowned sailors and their widows. This day had been marked by a special ceremony for ten years: ever since Albert had returned home with the news that their ship and all crew were lost. Everyone wore black to mourn the dead, and was entitled to take a day from work if they wanted. But for a service which Albert had practically started, he'd never attended it.

"On this anniversary of the sinking of the *Senara*, let us remember the unfortunates of both land and sea," said the vicar. "Let us remember how they set their course for the fishing grounds, only to be met with a danger that is unknown and unknowable. Let us remember the toll we suffered of this loss. We will not forget."

Florence tucked her arm in Connie's as they made their way home. Connie did her best to take the older woman's weight, since Dawn had disappeared to inquire about whether she could take on another job. The crowd filtered away, and Connie pulled off her bonnet so her dark curls could fall down her back.

"Do I need to ask whether you went or not?" Florence asked dryly.

Connie looked at her. "How do you know?"

"You will be a light sleeper too, when you get to my age. I saw you running off. Good thing it's summer, otherwise you might have caught your death. Mind, I'm surprised you *didn't* catch it, hearing the song."

Connie's eyes widened. "Yes!" she whispered. "I saw them! The mermaids! They were in the cove, two of them!"

Florence chuckled, wiping some spittle from her thin lips. "Be wary. They'll drag you with them. They tried to take your father, you know."

That brought back memories of the argument, and Connie sighed, busying herself with guiding Florence along the quay. The old woman began to sway with the rhythm of the boats, and threw her head back, cackling.

"Oh, yes, they sing and sing until you hear nothing else! They will blow up a storm, like they did with those poor sailormen!"

The villagers began throwing irritated glances. It was all Connie could manage to keep hold of Florence's flailing arms, before Dawn ran beside her to help. Together, they took Florence back to the house, but Connie's head swam with images of the moonlit cove, and the creatures sitting there.

She suddenly recalled the name of the young one. Heloise.

*

After changing out of her black dress, Connie ran to the fish market to buy their dinner. The stallholders usually closed up on the anniversary, but they couldn't today, since a catch had been brought in. Elbowing her way through the crowd, Connie selected two fat sides of cod, and paid with all of her mother's wages from the previous day. Then she walked straight home and set to work with the filleting knife, while Dawn scrubbed a pile of dirty clothes over a washboard.

Before long, the fish were cooking. As she buttered bread, Connie glanced over her shoulder to the window where Albert was sitting. But she didn't look at her father at all. From her angle, she could see over to the Leap, and the rocks at the bottom which marked the boundary of the little cove. The sun was hanging low, and transformed the sea into liquid gold.

As usual, all of them ate separate. Albert stayed in his chair; Florence in the back room; Dawn at the washtub as she struggled to finish her work. Connie stood in the corner underneath the drying herbs, holding her plate in one hand. She deliberately kept her back to the window, as though looking outside for too long would give away what she was planning.

The summer night seemed to take forever to draw in, and time felt even slower as Connie waited for the sound of her parents going to bed. She sat on her thin mattress, already dressed, tapping her heels impatiently on the floor. She'd chosen a dull brown frock which was practically the exact same shade as her hair, and so old, it never mattered if she dirtied it.

Eventually, silence fell, and she eased into the main room. She'd decided against going out the window again, in case Florence saw her and woke everybody. She went barefoot as before, to make as little noise as possible, but then she almost cried out when she saw the shape of her father still in the chair.

She froze, trying to wish herself into the shadows. Her heart rose into her throat. What would he say if he saw her out here? Would he send her back to bed, or throw her out like a piece of rubbish?

Then she noticed his breathing was steady; and his head bowed onto his heavy chest. Hands in anxious fists, she inched forward, craning her neck to see. To her relief, he was asleep, tongue protruding slightly from between his lips.

Moving quickly in case he woke, Connie darted past and lifted the latch. Instantly thankful that her mother kept it oiled, she opened the door a crack, crept outside, and shut it with barely a sound. Then she turned on her heel and sprinted away, past the creaking boats in the harbour. Adrenaline raced through her blood as the wind picked up, and then she heard it: the song.

She ran faster, leaving Trewhella behind. Stones and fragments of seashells embedded into her feet, but she didn't care. The Leap silhouetted itself against the moon as she reached the rocks, and drew to a halt, one hand on the nearest slab as she caught her breath.

Deep down, she was nervous they would flee again, but she knew she couldn't wait another second, and gently eased herself through the slippery teeth. The cove came into view, so she clung to a handhold, gazing towards the sea.

She couldn't see the mermaids anywhere. She even craned her neck around to where the younger one had been sitting the night before, but the place was barren. As though in double mockery, the wind stilled, and so did the song with it.

Connie's heart sank. Her fingers became numb from clutching the ledge, so she moved forward into the cove. She took herself over to the flat ledge where the older one had been, and perched on its edge, digging her toes into the sand. The tide was in, and with every soft wave, a little water pooled around her feet.

Disappointment bit at her insides and she lowered her head. Had she dreamed it all? Was she becoming as mad as Florence? The song she'd thought she had heard was nothing more than the wind, whistling through the rocks and down the streets. It wasn't the first time bizarre things had been heard on the coast; any who lived this close to the sea would attest to that. Strange things could play tricks in the periphery, and odd noises whisper in the ear. Nothing was ever quite what it seemed, here at the edge of the land.

"How can you hear me?"

Connie spun around so fast; she fell off the rock and into the surf. A wet patch spread on her back, but she barely felt it as her mouth dropped open in amazement.

The younger mermaid was in the water, just a few paces away. Her tail was submerged, and to anyone else, she might have looked simply like a human girl. But to Connie, there was no mistaking her.

"How do you hear my song?" the mermaid asked again. "Answer me."

"I... I don't know," Connie blurted. "I won't hurt you."

The mermaid tilted her head to the side like an inquisitive cat. "So it *is* you. The same one who came last night. You shouldn't have been able to hear us."

"I'm sorry. I haven't told anyone..." Connie broke off, remembering how she'd admitted it to Florence, but then assured herself that didn't count since nobody believed the old woman anyway. "Please, don't go. I came to see you again."

"Why?"

Connie didn't answer. Why had she come back? She couldn't think of a genuine answer. Her reasons were a knot of confusion inside her head, and she just stood there dumbly, staring.

The mermaid looked straight back. Her eyes were a piercing slate grey, and her long hair hung straight and wet over the front of her body. The starfish had moved across her scalp, and was now clinging to the top of her head like an obscure crown. One of its limbs extended over her forehead to just above her eye.

"Your name's Heloise, isn't it?" Connie asked. She stepped forward, but the mermaid immediately shied back, so she stopped, holding her hands out as if to calm a fretful animal. "Don't worry, I will not hurt you. I promise." She swallowed. "Where's... where's your mother?"

"She does not know I'm here." Heloise didn't move. "I came to sing by myself. To see if you would come again."

A jolt of apprehension seized Connie. Florence had warned her that mermaids would take her away if she went to the cove. They would lure their prey with songs, and then drag them into the deep, to never be seen again.

She was suddenly very aware of the Lover's Leap towering behind her, and remembered how it had got its name.

"Why are you afraid?" Heloise asked, but it was saturated with genuine confusion. "You are just a girl."

"Then why did you sing to me?" Connie snapped, trying to suppress her nerves.

"Children never come to the song of the ocean," said Heloise. "Only seafarers. That's what my mother told me. How did you hear us? How did you hear *me*?"

"I just did," Connie replied, with more impatience. "And it's a fishing village; all of us have the sea in our blood here. Is that wrong, that I heard it, even though I've never set foot on a ship? It's unlucky anyway, for a girl to go onboard."

"No. I'm just curious." Heloise paused. "I mean you no harm, like you've said you mean none to me. Please, let's just talk. Us two, now. What is your name?"

"Connie."

Heloise nodded; then proceeded to swim closer to the shore. Connie took a step back as the mermaid dug her fingers into the sand, using her arms to haul herself forward, until she reached the rocky slab her mother had been sitting on the night before. She leapt atop it with surprising agility, curling her tail around it like an anchor.

For the first time, Connie could see every detail of her. She was slender, but toned; her hair thinner than spider silk. There was no clear distinction between where her tail ended and flesh began. It looked like the silver of a dolphin, running gently into the colour of pale human skin. Her fins spanned wide, and curled inwards slightly as she flexed the muscles.

"How old are you?" Connie asked; wonder creeping back into her voice.

"Ten," said Heloise. "Are we the same age?"

Connie shook her head. "I'm a year older."

Heloise swept her hair over one shoulder, making the starfish constrict slightly around her scalp. Connie glanced at it; then noticed for the first time that the mermaid's hands were webbed, with thin skin stretching to the second knuckle of every finger.

"So, the song," Heloise said. "Please, explain how you came."

Connie shook her head, still in awe of the creature in front of her. "I just thought I heard voices on the wind. So I followed them, and you were both here." She sucked her lips into her mouth. "Hey, what were you doing here last night anyway? I've never heard of... people like you... around here."

"My mother came here to sing for the man she loves," replied Heloise simply. "I came to learn her song. So I can find someone to love, one day when I'm grown."

"Why didn't she just come into the harbour? She might have had a better chance of being heard," said Connie.

"With all those woven contraptions trailing in the water?" Heloise snorted. "Do you think we would ever manage return to sea?"

Offended by her haughty tone, Connie turned away and began dabbling her feet in the shallows. She didn't want to go home and ruin this opportunity, but she still stuck out her bottom lip irately.

"You are rude," she stated, watching a crab scuttling near her toes.

"I am truthful," returned Heloise, but the softness had returned.

"So am I," said Connie. Then she relented and looked back. "So you came tonight to see if I'd hear you again. Well, I did. So what does that say about me? Am I supposed to help your mother find who she seeks?"

"I do not know," Heloise admitted, flicking her tail so some water splashed over her lap.

"If you tell me his name, then I can say if he's still here. Maybe if he has moved away, that's why he didn't come to her."

"Alright. Mother told me he goes by Albert Marner."

Connie's eyes widened. "That's *my* name!"

Heloise cocked her head again in bewilderment. "What?"

"No, no, not like that!" Connie stammered. "I meant it's my surname: Marner! Albert Marner is my Papa."

At that, Heloise mirrored Connie's expression perfectly. Her pearly fingers gripped the rock so tight; her knuckles turned a pure white.

"He's mine, too!" the mermaid cried. "He is my mother's love!"

The two of them fell into silence. Only the whispers of the tide passed between them. Connie barely felt the water around her ankles anymore, or the serene coolness of the night. The entire world suddenly seemed to form a bell jar around them, disguised against the velvety sky, looking down to see what would happen now. And then, as though making a hairline crack, Connie forced words from her lips.

"So we have the same father?" She took a step closer. "Then... then you and I are..."

"Sisters?" Heloise finished, her own voice ringing with astonishment. "Half-sisters?"

"Is that possible?" Connie whispered. "I mean... I have legs; and you..."

"I don't know, but it would seem so." Heloise held a hand to her forehead. The fins on her hips shivered, and gave off such an alarming sound, Connie almost backed away again. It was like a hissing snake, or the noise of fish slithering over each other when the nets were hauled ashore.

But then, she realised she didn't care how it was possible. Even though a part of her ached to know, she couldn't help but remember her friendless childhood: devoid of so much affection and company. She could see the shipwreck orphans in her mind, always keeping clear of her, preferring to find comfort in a loss they all shared and which they believed she could never know. Albert's cruel words rang through her like a blade. All this time, he'd cut her off, and been the cause of all her loneliness – but yet because of him, she had flesh and blood; a sibling.

Dazed with the sudden sense of fondness, Connie moved forward and placed her hand on top of Heloise's. The mermaid glanced over her, as though shocked at being touched.

"You're so cold," Connie gasped, not sure what to say.

"No, you are hot!" Heloise pulled away, but not nastily. She looked genuinely taken aback at such a simple notion. "How can your flesh be so warm?"

Connie gave a small shake of her head, eyes still wide. "I don't know."

Then Heloise suddenly grinned, and reached back to her, grasping Connie's hand in both of hers. She flicked her tail again, unwinding it from the rock to curl around the other side.

"That must be why you heard me," she whispered. "My blood is in your veins. The blood of the ocean runs in both of us."

Connie returned the smile until her cheeks ached. "So we are sisters," she breathed.

"I believe we are, yes," said Heloise. "I see it now, how you look like me. We have the same nose."

The two of them chuckled. Connie raised her hand, and then her other one. Heloise took the hint and released her, so they could both press their fingers together. They drew closer, until their foreheads were almost touching, with the happiness still lighting up their faces.

"I never thought to have a sister here," Heloise whispered.

"Or a friend, for me," added Connie.

"*I* shall be your friend, Connie Marner," the mermaid assured confidently. "I will be your dearest friend forever."

Connie laughed. "Yes, and I will be the same to you, Heloise Marner. I promise."

Chapter  Three

When Connie returned home, a renewed vigour was racing in her body, and she had to remind herself not to make too much noise. Albert was still asleep in his chair, so she sneaked past him before shutting herself in her room.

She perched on her bed in the darkness, hugging her knees and staring excitedly at her teddy. Unable to still, she rocked back and forth for a few minutes before lighting the candle on her nightstand. She snatched a stubby pencil and crinkled sheet of paper; then balanced a book on her lap to lean on. Working quickly, before the tiny wick could splutter out, she scribbled a picture of Heloise, sitting on the rock with her hair blowing.

Desperate to capture the mermaid's image before she forgot any detail, Connie meticulously sketched the starfish on her scalp; the way her fins curled inwards around the dark slab.

Eventually, as she was crazily drawing some waves on the water, the candle died and plunged her back into the gloom. Connie growled in frustration, but nevertheless stuck her picture on a nail protruding from a plank in the wall. Then she settled down against her pillow and tried to force her eager heart to slow. The prospect of work tomorrow barely crossed her mind before exhaustion suddenly overwhelmed her, and she fell into a deep sleep.

When she next opened her eyes, she was still in the same position, and early light was filtering in through the thin curtains. Instantly awake, she made her bed and tied her unruly hair with a pink ribbon, before heading into the main room. Albert was still slumbering, which Connie immediately put down to a hangover. There was no sign of Dawn or Florence, but the village was a hive of activity, and Connie only needed to take one look outside to see one of the fishing ships being prepared in the harbour.

Chewing on a slice of bread, she wandered to the quay, and watched as the sailors ran about shouting orders. She instantly knew there must be a large school of fish somewhere nearby. The catches had been getting smaller and smaller with each year, and there was only a rush like this if the fishermen knew they had a limited window of opportunity to make a good haul. It would be a race to seize the fish before they moved too far away.

Connie stayed until the ship was on its way, the white sails full with a strong wind. As it disappeared between the breakwaters, she suddenly remembered what Heloise had said about the fishing nets; how they could stop a mermaid returning to sea. Connie silently hoped her sister would stay clear of the vessel. She wanted to be able to see her again tonight.

The idea of Heloise as her sister sang in Connie's mind. For the first time, she was not alone. And, of all the brilliant and fantastical things, she shared blood with a *mermaid!*

It was still hanging there like a dream, somewhere deep inside her, as she made her way to the church, practically skipping every step in her joy. The little building was empty even of the vicar, but she didn't want any company. She walked straight up the aisle to the altar, and looked properly at the old carving for the first time.

It was relatively large: about the length of her arm, and positioned firmly between the stones of the wall. The surface was smooth, as though it had been engraved in a piece of driftwood. Framed by stylised waves and leaping fish, sat the mermaid, with her tail curling and arms raised as though in greeting.

Connie's eyes widened with wonder. The wooden woman didn't just look like Heloise. It bore a striking resemblance to the other one: her mother.

*

When Connie returned home, Dawn was awake and had already started on the day's laundry. Connie immediately joined her, taking the clothes to press through the mangle.

She glanced at Dawn's hands. They had been pink and puckered for years, from constant submergence in the soapy water. Her skin had become thin and aged prematurely, with liver spots appearing even though Dawn was barely into her forties.

Not saying a word, Connie's eyes wandered to her mother's face. She kept herself turned to the mangle so Dawn wouldn't notice her staring, but still bit her lip in dismay. Dawn's cheeks were pale and her brown hair was oddly limp, falling out of its natural curls until it hung like wet straw across her shoulders. Dark circles had puffed under her eyes, and Connie noticed how unsure her movements suddenly seemed.

The argument fleeted in Connie's mind. Had it dealt a deeper blow to her mother than she'd first thought? She was definitely slowing down, and every now and then, she would sniff deeply, as though a sickness was trying to wedge itself in her sinuses.

Dawn tipped some more soap into the basin. Its strong odour flew up Connie's nose and made her eyes water. Even though she was used to the effects, she wiped clumsily at her face with the hem of her sleeve.

"Are you alright, dear?" Dawn asked, her voice sounding as flat as her hair.

Connie swallowed down a sob. "Yes, Mama."

"Oh, your ribbon looks beautiful. I didn't notice it before."

Connie didn't say anything, but she knew Dawn hadn't noticed because this was the first time her mother had looked at her all morning. She never ignored her like this, like Albert did. Something was wrong.

"Do you feel well?" Connie inquired gently.

Dawn gave a tight smile that told her not to press further. "Of course. Now be a dear and make a tea for Granny Florence."

Pursing her lips anxiously, Connie brewed some water and tea leaves over the fire. She lifted the kettle off the hook; poured the contents into Florence's flask, and then took it into the back room. The old lady was asleep in the rocking chair, mouth gaping like a fish. Knowing waking her would result in a rant, Connie decided not to disturb her. She placed the tea on the nearby table; then returned to her mother.

Remembering how Dawn had been searching for more work after the anniversary service, Connie bade a hasty goodbye and then ran down to the marketplace, where the fishmongers were busying themselves cleaning mussels and cockles. They were from local stocks, but lower fare compared to the bony fish of the outer seas. Connie knew the vendors were getting ready for shellfish sales, in case the ship returned with empty nets.

She went from stall to stall, asking everyone if they were willing to take her on as a part-time apprentice. It would be meagre money, but meant Dawn could at least sleep a little better at night. However, despite using her sweetest voice and smoothing her skirt until it fell perfectly, none of the stallholders offered her a job. They all shook their heads with a small smile, before waving her off like a bothersome kitten.

Even though none of them said it, Connie knew why they were turning her away. She could see the dislike in their eyes; the knowledge of whose daughter she was. In her, all they noticed was the surly drunkard who had indirectly driven the widows to their deaths.

The silent accusations felt worse than if they had been shouted in her face. Connie hid behind a wall near the quay, trying to force herself not to cry.

At that moment, a group of children came bustling along the steep street. The sound of them laughing at some joke made her look up. They were all of a similar age to her, and she recognised some of them as being *Senara* orphans. When they glanced at her, she offered a polite smile; hoping that this time, they would return the gesture and invite her along. But no such thing happened. They shuffled past with the usual cold stares, all keeping a wide berth so she couldn't even reach over and tap them on the shoulder.

It was nothing out of the ordinary, but as they disappeared round the corner, it suddenly broke something inside Connie. She ground her teeth together, felt her hands curl into fists. Frustration boiled in her blood. It was so unfair, that her own life should be poisoned by her father. It wasn't enough that he'd ignored her; his very influence made everybody else stay clear of her as though she was an infected animal.

At last, angry tears spilled down her cheeks. Covering her face wretchedly, Connie sprinted away from Trewhella, up the hill, until she was at the summit of the Lover's Leap. Then she flung herself on the grass and cried until she couldn't anymore.

Chapter Four

She didn't go home for dinner. In the back of her mind, she knew Dawn would be wondering where she was, but it still wasn't enough to make Connie return. Too overcome with her own problems, she pushed everyone else from her thoughts. Alone, watching the day melt into night, she decided firmly that this time now belonged to her, for once.

When her stomach began to grumble, she wandered into the little woodland at the rear of the Leap, and found a strawberry bush. Filling her apron, she went back into the open and ate them, tossing the green stalks over the cliff.

All the while, she kept her eyes fixed on the silvery water, waiting for Heloise. The evening before, the two of them had agreed to meet again at midnight. The hours dragged by, as though sensing Connie's anticipation, and when the moon eventually drew to its highest point, she could barely stay still.

When she thought she couldn't wait another minute, she saw a definite silhouette rise out of the water. Connie let out a squeal of excitement, and raced down the Leap with such speed, she almost fell flat on her face. She pushed herself through the rocks into the cove, to find Heloise already there, sitting on the slab.

"You came!" Connie laughed, settling herself beside the mermaid.

"Of course I did," said Heloise, but her last word was muffled as Connie pulled her into a hug.

Heloise stiffened a little at the sudden movement, but then returned the gesture, placing her hands on Connie's back. Then she noticed the pink ribbon in Connie's hair, and began playing with it in fascination.

"How are you?" Connie asked when they drew apart. The embrace had left her sleeves sodden, so she rolled them up until the cuffs were at her elbows.

"I'm well," Heloise replied, still stroking the ribbon. "What about you?"

Connie gave a despondent shrug, but decided her struggles were not going to ruin this one escape.

"I went to the markets for a job," she said instead, "but nobody wanted me."

Heloise tilted her head. "What's a... job?"

"You know, work." Connie frowned. "Don't you have jobs where you come from?"

"We sing," Heloise offered. "Does that count?"

"If it's what you do every day, then I suppose it does," said Connie.

"Then what do *you* do every day? Don't you sing?"

"I know a few sea shanties, but you can't really do much with singing here. It's not practical. You've got to do something for the village. My Mama washes clothes, so I help her."

Heloise stretched her tail out and leaned closer to Connie. "Sea shanties? I've heard the sailormen singing those. Oh, sing one for me! I might know it!"

Connie instantly felt shy. Nobody had ever mentioned whether she had a nice voice or not, but she knew it would be horrendous compared to the beauty of Heloise and her mother. Heloise was insistent however, so Connie relented.

"Have you heard the news, me Johnny?

One more day!

We're homeward bound tomorrow.

Only one more day!

Don't you hear the old man growlin'?

One more day!

Don't you hear the mate a-howlin'?

Only one more day!"

As Connie had feared, Heloise immediately pulled a face at her tone, but then hid it quickly and began singing with her. Overjoyed that Heloise knew the shanty, Connie raised her voice as much as she dared.

"No more gales or heavy weather.

One more day!

Only one more day together.

Only one more day!"

By the time they had finished, both sisters were smiling widely. They moved closer, until their temples were touching and arms linked. Giggling gently, Connie gazed at Heloise's sleek tail, slightly distorted by the waves lapping around the rock. She gathered up her skirt so the material wouldn't get wet, and then slipped her feet into the water beside the silvery fins.

"You know, there's a mermaid carving in the church in the village," she said, copying Heloise's movements with her toes. "It's been there for ages."

Heloise was silent for a moment, and Connie guessed she was thinking over all these new words which were being thrown at her.

"Is it a figurehead?" Heloise asked. "I've seen those on the ship prows."

"No, it's just a flat piece of wood. It looks a lot like your mother."

"It could well be. She's old."

"How old is she?"

"Actually, I'm not sure. I just know she's old."

Connie wondered how it was possible to not know a parent's age, but was distracted when Heloise began prodding at the starfish. It was near the base of her skull tonight, and she eased it around until it was wrapping around her ear.

"I saw a fishing ship today," said Heloise. "It's from your village."

"Yes. I was hoping you wouldn't get caught." Connie twiddled her thumbs. "Take care. They'll have a lot of nets."

"I will," Heloise smiled. "Mermaids can die if we are trapped in nets, you see. We're like dolphins; we need to breathe air."

"Your tail looks like a dolphin's," Connie observed, gently running her hand over it. She marvelled at the feeling of it: firm and muscular, but yet smooth, like stretched rubber.

"If you ever got caught in a net, I'd get you out," she muttered. "I wouldn't let you die."

Heloise chuckled. "That's kind of you."

"Well, you'd never let the sea kill *me*, would you?" Connie said, meeting her sister's eyes expectantly.

"Of course not," Heloise whispered, a gentle smile on her lips. Then she wrapped a cool arm around Connie's back. "So, do you have any other siblings, on the land?"

"No." Connie sighed. "What about you?"

"I do," said Heloise. "I have eight other sisters, but they're all older than me. Much older. None of us are the same age. Not like you and me."

"Eight sisters!" Connie exclaimed, feeling her eyes widening. "Do you see them often?"

"Sometimes. I stay with my mother more than any of them." Heloise turned her eyes back to the sea, and they sparkled like stars. "My sisters and mother used to have free reign of the ocean. Every seafarer knew of them, and treated them like goddesses. It's not the same today, or so they tell me."

Connie followed the line of Heloise's gaze. She trailed her feet in the water, sweeping some sand with her toes and watching it form a billowing cloud before settling again.

Heloise suddenly glanced at her with a spark of determination. "I know! Let's go swimming! Come out with me! I'll show you the seabed!"

Connie's pulse sped up in excitement and fright.

"I can't!" she spluttered. "I don't know how to swim."

"You can't swim?" Heloise repeated incredulously. "But you live right here on the coast!"

"I've never been in past my knees," Connie mumbled.

"Well, we will have to do something about that!" declared Heloise. She let go of Connie and slipped off the rock, until she was sitting on the sand and the waves washed around her chest. She held out her arms beckoningly.

"You'll be safe with me," she urged. "I'll show you what to do."

Connie hesitated. "I honestly won't get hurt?"

"I promise," Heloise said. "Come on! We won't go far."

Connie swallowed, but felt reassured, and stood so she could pull her dress over her head. She folded it into a neat pile and left it out of reach of the waves, until she was wearing nothing but her white chemise. Heloise helped her down, Connie grasping the mermaid's wrist, unable to hold her hand because of the webbing between her fingers.

Heloise slowly guided her deeper, until the water rose past Connie's knees and to her waist. Connie's heart began to beat hard, but one look at Heloise's composed smile chased all fear away. She was in her sister's element now, and the two of them had promised they would never let the other come to harm. She was safe.

Staying close, Heloise urged Connie to lift her feet off the bottom. She did, and immediately sunk up to her neck. Panic surged and she went to thrust her legs down, but Heloise swept her tail beneath Connie to keep her afloat.

"Relax," the mermaid muttered. "Look at what I'm doing."

The moonlight reflected off her tail, and Connie watched its movements, waving gently back and forth. Realising the joints were in exactly the same place as her own knees and ankles, Connie brought her legs together in a mimic, copying until she felt her weight disappear into the water.

"I'm doing it!" she cried excitedly.

"Well done," Heloise smiled. "Now, flip onto your belly, and put your other hand out in front."

Connie did as she was told, and Heloise pulled her further out, until the sand was too deep for her to stand. She struggled to keep her head above the water, and spluttered whenever a wave smacked into her face, but Heloise whispered constant comfort. Her words brought a strange serenity to Connie, helping her calm down.

"I don't think you'll be able to hold your breath for as long as me," said Heloise. "Tap me on the arm when you need to come up."

"Alright."

Filling her lungs with oxygen, Connie nodded to show she was ready; then Heloise plunged with her under the surface. A stream of bubbles tickled Connie's face as they descended, and the water stung her eyes terribly, but she squinted through the discomfort until it subsided. Everything was blurry and half-shrouded in shadows, but milky bars of moonlight were dancing through from above, and she could just make out the shifting patterns on the seabed below.

Heloise threw her a thrilled grin, moving deeper with one powerful stroke of her tail. The pressure closed around Connie's chest, but she held onto her breath, determined to make it last.

She hadn't been sure about what being underwater would be like, but it certainly wasn't like this. She felt as though she was caught in a soft weightless embrace, surrounded by one long moment, separate from the rest of the world. It was unbelievably comfortable, and she soon lost all sense of time.

Her body began to protest, and she put her hand on Heloise's arm to tell her she needed air. Heloise immediately darted for the surface, and barely a second later, they appeared back into the night.

"It's beautiful!" Connie gasped. "Just beautiful!"

"I know," smiled Heloise, but her eyebrows were raised in disbelief. "I didn't think you could only last that long. I can hold it for fifteen minutes – that was barely one!"

Connie flustered. "Sorry. I've never done this before."

"I'll bear it in mind, so I don't take you too deep," Heloise assured. "Are you ready?"

Connie nodded, and the two of them dived again, with Heloise moving quicker so they could reach the seabed. Connie copied her stroke, flicking her legs back and forth from the hips. Mermaid and girl drew close, foreheads touching gleefully, as their hair billowed in the currents.

Heloise pulled her down until their bellies were rubbing along the sand; then started to skim the bottom like a hunting seal. Before long, she grabbed something, and held it up so Connie could see. Connie narrowed her eyes, trying to make it out from the blur of colour, but shook her head regretfully before pointing upwards. Heloise duly returned to the surface, supporting Connie with one arm as she gulped air.

"Here," Heloise said, thrusting the thing into Connie's hand.

Connie looked at it, able to see clearly now. It was a small conch shell, pale pink in colour, with a small twist at the top above the gaping hole. It wasn't anything unusual; this kind of shell often washed up on the beaches. But while most were smashed or dull-looking, this one seemed covered with a perfect glaze.

"Put it to your ear," said Heloise.

Connie did, and was shocked to hear the sound of the sea from inside the shell. It wavered and lifted like mermaid song, only to disappear when she lowered it.

"If you do that," Heloise smiled, "you'll always hear the ocean. No matter how far inland you go, it will stay with you."

Connie hugged her awkwardly, treading water as best she could. She tucked the shell into the neck of her chemise for safekeeping, then pulled the pink ribbon free. Letting go of Heloise so she could paddle behind her, Connie threaded the pink silk through her sister's hair, and tied it in a little bow.

"There," she said. "It looks lovely on you."

Heloise explored the ribbon with interest, running it through her fingers like she had before. Her movements disturbed the starfish and it crawled onto her temple to keep out of the way.

The sisters looked at each other fondly, and Connie leaned in to kiss Heloise on the cheek. Heloise touched her face softly before returning the gesture.

"Come," she whispered. "Let me show you some speed!"

Connie only had time to snatch a breath before Heloise pulled her under again and shot through the water like an arrow. Connie bit her lips together to stop herself screaming elatedly. Her hair streaked straight along her back, and the sea opened up ahead: an endless playground just for the two of them.

Chapter  Five

They stayed together for hours, with the stars spinning through the sky overhead, laughing and splashing one another at the mouth of the cove. Heloise dived in and out of the water like a playful dolphin; raised her tail above the surface to wave the fin at Connie. Time lost all meaning for them, and it was only when Connie looked up to see how far the moon had moved west that she insisted she should head home. Heloise helped her return to shore, promising to wait for her tomorrow at the same hour, before disappearing under the waves.

The night air chilled Connie through her soaking chemise, so she wrung out the thin material as best she could, then she slipped her dress back on. The material clung to her body uncomfortably, and it felt strange to be on her feet again, so she took her time squeezing through the rocks onto the flats. Still trembling with delight, she made her way to the village.

The streets were deserted, so Connie didn't bother keeping in the shadows. Eventually, she rounded the corner and hurried up the path to her front door, but froze when she saw a hunched figure sitting on the step.

"Well, well, well," Florence chuckled. "What have we here?"

"Granny!" Connie gasped. "What... why are you outside at this time? You'll catch a cold!"

Florence scoffed, eyeing her sodden dress. "*I'll* catch a cold, will I?"

Connie clasped her hands together nervously. The water had seeped through from her chemise, and now every inch of her clothes seemed ten times heavier. There was definitely no hiding it now.

"You've been very naughty," said Florence. "Your mother was beside herself with worry, when you didn't come home for dinner."

"I... I wasn't hungry."

"Mm. It's not good to swim on a full stomach, is it?"

"I can't swim!" Connie flustered.

Florence shook her head. "I told you already, you can't lie to me. And don't dig yourself deeper by saying you're not lying. I know a fib when I hear one, lass."

Connie looked at her feet despondently. "How did you know? Did you see me?"

"You only get that wet on a clear night by swimming, silly girl. I'm not as stupid as you think. And what's more, I know you've been with mermaids."

Connie's eyes shot up. "What?"

"You can't swim. You told me that yourself, a few years ago," said Florence. "Why else would you go out of your comfort zone unless you were absolutely captivated? That's just what they do."

"Granny, how can you remember me saying that to you?" Connie asked quietly. "You were having a fit."

Florence's face suddenly softened. "Listen, lass. I'm no madder than any old woman coming to the end of her life. You all just think I'm demented, and I let you get on with it, for my own fun. When you get to my age, you'll understand. It's all you can do, when you belong to a world that is slipping away into the pages of history."

Connie looked at her, unsure of what to make of it. This was the most lucid she'd ever seen Florence, through all the years she had been a part of the family. But there was a certainty in her words which Connie hadn't heard before. She found she wasn't anxious that Florence would abruptly relapse and start shrieking; but instead felt intrigued, and even a little sympathetic.

Seeing she had the girl's attention, Florence leaned forwards with a small smile. "It was different when I was your age. Back then, in the last century, everyone knew the mermaids existed, and treated them with respect. But times have moved on, and people have become too full of themselves. What with all these new inventions and things... they think they've risen above anything except what they call common sense. That's left no room for the old ways, or the people who know about them."

"Like you?" said Connie.

"Yes, like me," Florence replied with a snigger. "I've lived in this village all my life. I've seen it grow and change, and I heard mermaid song on the wind. You know, the widows of the *Senara* eleven years ago – they weren't the first to jump from the Leap."

"Really? But... I thought that was how it got its name, Lovers Leap!"

"Oh, no. It was called that long ago. But everyone only remembers that wreck because it was the first time the mermaids had struck for many years. It wasn't the first ship to be sunk by mermaid song, and the widows were just the latest in a long line who've followed their husbands to the bottom of the sea."

Connie put a hand to her mouth. Mermaids had been behind the *Senara*'s sinking? The event which weighed on her life since the day she was born?

Her thoughts flitted back to Heloise, and then to that first night, when Connie had seen both her and her mother singing on the wind. Could they know something about it? If Connie went to Heloise with these new questions, could she perhaps get some answers to the mystery?

A bout of suppressed coughing from Florence snapped her from her wonderings. She gazed deep into the old woman's sharp eyes, seeing a wry light of knowledge reflected in them.

"I overheard Mama and Papa arguing a few nights back," she admitted, barely above a whisper. "He does not love me. I heard it from his own mouth. He doesn't want me."

Florence snorted a laugh. "Even the pilchard-fish in stargazy pie could see that."

The abrupt cold words struck Connie's heart, and she bit her lip, trying to force tears back. But then Florence shook her head with a lopsided smirk, and stood, putting her twiggy arms around Connie. The hug took Connie by surprise, but she buried her face in Florence's chest, glad for the affection.

"Now, now, I'm only messing, lass," Florence muttered. "Old habits, you know. Don't you worry; it will all turn out alright in the end."

"I don't know," Connie admitted. "He doesn't love me. And Mama is so sad."

"Well, we can at least make sure she has less work to do," Florence said, cupping Connie's face in her hands. "If we wash that dress out now, no-one will notice it in the morning."

*

By the time they had cleaned the dress and chemise, the sun was close to rising, and Connie knew there would be no point sleeping now. So she stayed awake, saw Florence to bed with a flask of tea; then changed into a clean frock. She wrestled a comb through her tangled hair, and placed the conch shell atop her nightstand.

She checked the herbs in the rafters; visited the neighbours to buy some fresh eggs, and heated water for the clothes basin. She was fetching the broom when Albert staggered in and began rummaging through a cupboard for his gin.

Connie glanced at him. "Where is Mama?"

"Taken ill," Albert grunted. "You'll have to do all the work today."

"Yes, Papa," Connie mumbled.

She kept out of his way and quickly swept around his chair while the space was free. Wiping sweat from her brow, she returned to the closet for the dustpan and brush, knelt beside the pile of dirt to clean it up.

"I'm out. None left," Albert said, shutting the cupboard loudly. "Go into the village and get me some more."

Connie froze, the dustpan twitching in her hand. "We don't have enough money spare. Mama hasn't been paid yet."

"Do as you're told!" snapped Albert. His eyes were flat with panic for the lack of alcohol, which quickly flashed to anger in an attempt to hide it. It was a terrifying cocktail. Connie felt adrenaline moving into her blood. But then, the flight transformed into fight, and she got to her feet.

"Your legs aren't broken, Papa. Go for it yourself."

The words were out of her mouth before she could stop them. Albert drew himself up to his full height, face turning the colour of beetroot.

"You will not talk that way to me!" he shouted.

"Stop ordering me around!" Connie cried, her patience snapped. "And leave Mama alone! You're always so mean to us and it's not fair! You never leave any money for us because you make us buy all your gin! Stop it!"

"Silence!" Albert roared. "You will do as I tell you, girl!"

"I will not!" Connie screamed back.

Albert's hand flew out. Connie barely felt the sting on her face before she crashed to the ground. Trembling with fright, she felt her nose, and her fingers came away red.

She pressed herself against the wall as Albert rummaged around for Dawn's coin purse. Shaking out the meagre few pennies, he stormed away, without as much as a look back.

Connie stayed there for a few minutes longer, coming down from the shock. Her face smarted with pain, but she forced herself to ignore it, moving gingerly to the basin so she could wash herself. Blood ran freely from her nose, so she pinched the bridge between her fingers, holding a handkerchief above her lips to soak up the excess. When the bleeding ceased, she splashed some cold water on her face to cool the pain.

Albert returned before long, bottle in hand, and collapsed into his chair. Neither of them spoke, and whenever Connie caught him glancing at her, she turned the other way. She finished her work as quickly as she could, boiled the kettle in the fireplace, and made some tea which she duly took to her mother.

Dawn looked terrible. Her face was pale and eyes dark, her breaths rattling. Connie could tell it wasn't anything too serious, but it seemed worse because of how exhausted she knew her mother was. Dawn coughed as Connie came in, and propped herself up on the pillows so she could take the tea.

"Thank you, dear," she said, managing a small smile. "Where were you last night?"

"I wasn't hungry," Connie replied. It was the first thing she'd said since losing control, and talking around her throbbing cheek was strangely difficult.

"Did you go for a walk?" Dawn asked. She took a sip of the tea and set the flask on the nightstand.

"Yes. Sorry. I lost track of the time."

"Don't do it again. You had me worried."

"Yes, Mama."

"Oh!" Dawn suddenly cried, reaching out to Connie. "What happened to your face? Your cheek's all bruised!"

Realising with both dismay and relief that her mother hadn't heard the fight, Connie just shook her head, and replied that she'd simply tripped and fallen into the doorframe.

Chapter  Six

The day dragged by, with Connie working as hard as she could to keep on top of her mother's workload. It wasn't the first time she'd stood in for Dawn falling ill, but now it seemed to hold a heavier weight than before. She almost felt like she was still wearing her wet dress, with the fabric pulling on her shoulders and hips, surrounding her in a puddle of dripping water.

After making a pot of mussel broth for everyone's dinner, Connie took herself to bed and curled up wretchedly with her teddy bear. Her cheek had swollen throughout the afternoon, and the initial pain lessened until it formed a constant dull ache. She grimaced whenever she touched it, imagining the bruise which would form overnight.

For as exhausted as she was, she only let herself catch a few hours' sleep before she awoke again, dressed, and slipped outside. The moon was on the wane into its crescent shape, but still casting enough light to see by. Connie followed it out of Trewhella, moving slowly, unable to find the energy to run. Even her usual excitement to see Heloise was dim tonight.

When she eventually pushed herself through into the cove, she was surprised to find Heloise already waiting for her, sitting on the rock.

"You're late," the mermaid noted.

"I fell asleep," said Connie as she approached. A yawn crept up on her and she raised a hand to cover her mouth, accidentally brushing against her cheek. She winced, and Heloise noticed immediately.

"You're injured!" Heloise cried, pulling Connie down beside her. "What happened?"

"Nothing," Connie said quickly. "It doesn't hurt much."

"What did you do?"

"I didn't do anything. I don't want to talk about it."

Heloise held Connie's eyes for another few seconds, but then nodded and let the matter drop. Connie wiped her nose gently, and noticed that Heloise was still wearing the pink ribbon in her hair.

"Connie," Heloise said, "do you remember, last night, you said if I was ever in trouble with nets, you'd get me free?"

Connie frowned, looking over her sister's immaculate tail. "Yes... but, why? You're not trapped in any."

"No, my mother is." Heloise clutched at Connie's hands earnestly. "If I bring her, would you help? Please?"

"Of course," replied Connie, surprised that she'd have to make good on her promise so soon. "I will do what I can."

Heloise hugged her in gratitude; then slipped off the rock and under the waves without another word. She disappeared for a few minutes, and then resurfaced with another mermaid at her side. Connie stood and went to wade into the water to help, but remembered the fuss of trying to wash her dress from the night before. So she waited until Heloise and her mother were nearer the shallows. Then she grasped the older mermaid's wrists, pulling her up the beach with Heloise pushing behind.

The three of them stopped near the strandline. Connie knelt, looking over the damage, and swallowed nervously. The mermaid's silvery tail was cocooned in thick fishing twine, pressing fins into her hips. The rope had already cut deeply and bruised the sleek skin. It snaked around her belly and over one shoulder, with one of the ball-like weights still attached.

"Can you get her out of it?" Heloise asked anxiously. "I tried, but I couldn't get hold of it properly." She raised a hand and spread her webbed fingers in explanation.

"I think so," Connie said. "It will take a while to unwind though. I don't have a knife or anything."

"It was my own fault," the older mermaid sighed. "I got too close when they cast the nets. It was the ship that set out from here a few days ago."

Connie glanced at her, and then threw a questioning look at Heloise. "Does she know about us?"

"Yes, I do," replied Heloise's mother. "Albert mentioned to me that he had a child due back home, but I never thought I'd meet you, Connie."

She smiled, showing a set of perfectly aligned white teeth. "My name is Raniira."

Connie felt her heart skip a beat with recognition. Raniira was the name Albert had mentioned in the argument with her mother. It was the one who he truly loved.

She remained silent as she worked at the nets, forcing her fingers through the twine. It took a long time to unwind them, and she made a wrong turn more than once, but didn't give up, and soon, the heavy ropes fell away onto the sand.

Raniira carefully eased her tail free, waving it in the air to get blood flowing. Heloise breathed an audible sigh of relief, and Connie fell back into a sitting position, now mentally exhausted as well as physically.

"Thank you, child," said Raniira, rubbing the sore patches of flesh. "You truly are a kind-hearted one."

Connie shrugged nonchalantly, but couldn't stop a smile at hearing the praise. Such words had never been given freely to her, even by Dawn. It formed a peculiar tingling warmth in her belly as she looked at the mermaid.

Only now that she saw Raniira up close, did she notice truly how uncannily she resembled the carving in the church. She was beautiful, even though age showed in her features; with barely a wrinkle or spot in sight. Her fine blonde hair was laced with white, and some skin was peeling at the base of her tail, but her eyes were alight with life, and the same strange power Connie noticed in Heloise.

"Thank you," Heloise said sincerely, tapping Connie's ankle from where she was lying on her belly in the shallows. "I knew I could count on you."

"It's no problem," Connie returned, still grinning. Then she turned to Raniira and asked, "How did you get tangled up? Did they catch you by surprise?"

Raniira chuckled. "In a way. They went for a large school of fish – too large. I tried singing, to direct them to a smaller one, but they didn't listen and I drew too close. It's very rare to find sailormen who care to listen anymore."

Connie frowned. "Like our father listened?"

Heloise's eyes flickered to Connie with an unreadable expression, but she still pulled herself closer and curled her tail; flicking the fins back and forth, like a human would sway their legs. Raniira stroked her daughter's shoulders gently, but didn't move her attention from Connie.

"Let me explain some lore to you," said the mermaid. "The respect given to us by the fishermen of old was a mutual respect. It allowed us to aid with their catches, guiding them. They brought home a good amount every year, and everyone with seafarer ways could hear our songs, so they would know when mermaids were near. If the respect was given, we would help them. If they scorned us, we would sing up a storm."

It reminded Connie of what Florence had said the night before. She smoothed her skirts, brushing off the sand which had gathered in the fabric.

"So where does Albert Marner come into it?"

"We are not beyond love, my dear," Raniira explained with a smile. "As payment for good nature, whenever a mermaid falls in love with a human, she can sing just for him. Over the years, I have borne nine daughters to sailormen, including Heloise. And all but one of the fathers has joined me in the depths after our night together. Albert Marner is the only one who returned to land, but I do still long for him. So I still sing the song, hoping he'll hear it someday."

Connie's hands writhed in her lap. "So what about the *Senara*, eleven years ago? Is that where you met him?"

"It was indeed," replied Raniira. "The crew had been disrespectful, by sailing straight past the fish we offered. Instead, they headed further out to sea, to pursue a whale. My elder daughters became offended and blew up a storm to drown the men. The sea foamed and boiled; the waves grew higher than the mainsail mast. The vessel went down in less than half an hour and all on board were thrown into the water.

"But I had seen one man, who tried to stop the turn of events. He insisted they leave the whale and just bring back their catch. None of the others wanted to listen to him, and my daughters were too incensed to take note. I felt a pull for him in my heart, so I sang to him through the storm, but the weather was too powerful.

"He was one of the last off the ship and would have drowned with the others, but I searched for him, rescued him and swam with him to the nearest shore. I pressed down on his chest to get the water out of his lungs;

breathed into his mouth to give him the kiss of life. When he woke, I stayed with him, and we didn't leave each other's side for three days. We were in love."

Heloise tilted her head in her usual fashion, drawing swirls into the sand with a tip of her finger. Connie watched her carve shells and seahorses; then move her hand away as the waves swept forward to fill the grooves she'd made.

"So... why didn't he stay with you?" Connie asked, finally coming to the question which had been haunting her. "Why did he come home, if you were so happy?"

Raniira gave her a soft look, as though trying to judge how much she should say. But Connie's eyes were insistent, and the mermaid finally relented, gently placing one of her webbed hands over the girl's.

"I pleaded with Albert to join me under the sea. But he felt terribly guilty, because he knew he had a wife and child back on the land. So he returned to his village."

It was a short and sweet answer, but held more weight than Connie had been expecting. She could see in Raniira's eyes, how much the mermaid was still enamoured with her father. And she didn't need to think twice, how often she had noticed the same longing in Albert's eyes, as he spent his days staring out the window at the sea.

For the first time, Connie realised the truth behind his apathy. It wasn't just the fact that he was bound in marriage to Dawn – she was sure that before his ill-fated voyage, her parents were very much in love. But the life he returned to after his time with Raniira was so mundane and unappealing that it had killed his zest for life. He had followed duty rather than heart, and it simply hadn't been enough.

Soon, Raniira announced that she would leave, to let the sisters have their usual time together. She hugged Connie again and gave Heloise a kiss on the cheek, before crawling back into the sea. She gave them a final flick of her tail in farewell; then vanished into the depths.

Heloise dug up some wet sand and began rolling it into a ball between her palms. Connie turned her eyes to the waves, watching how the moonlight moved on their crests. She found herself a little sad for her father. But then she felt the pain in her cheek and nose, and it was joined by fury that he'd still taken his own sadness out on her. It hadn't been her fault that his life wasn't what he wanted. No matter the reasons, and how much easier it might be for her to understand them, the fact remained that he had denied her happiness; destroyed her childhood. She would not let him destroy her future.

"So..." she said, "anyone used to be able to hear the song, huh?"

"Well, it seems that way," replied Heloise, flattening the sand-ball into a patty. "I still love how you heard me, though."

"Does that mean that anyone who a mermaid sings to can go away with them?"

"I suppose."

Connie looked at her, and reached over to catch her attention. "Take me with you."

Heloise froze. "What?"

"Take me to sea with you," Connie pleaded, her voice growing more determined with every word. "If I could hear the song, then I can leave the land, can't I? You want to know why I'm hurt? Papa hit me. He doesn't love me at all. I don't have a family, not like you do, Heloise. Please, please, let me come with you!"

Heloise held her eyes. "No. I can't."

"You can!" insisted Connie, feeling tears forming. "You don't know how unhappy I am; how happy you make me! Take me under the sea, please."

"No, I won't do it," said Heloise firmly. "There's no way we can ever be together in one world. I will never take you away from here."

Connie clasped her wrists tighter. "But we're sisters!"

"I know. But that doesn't change anything. You are human and I am mermaid."

Disappointment filled Connie's mind. Suddenly her face barely hurt anymore over the pain she felt in her heart. Even though they had only known each other for three days, already it seemed like a lifetime; and that she could trust her sister above all others.

Angry tears flowed freely and she scrambled to her feet, stalking away towards the back of the cove.

"It's not fair!" she cried, kicking sand with each step.

Heloise straightened up in alarm. "Connie, I cannot do anything about it!"

"You could have said yes!" Connie turned on her. "You're lucky; you don't know what it's like. Did you ever stop to think it's better to have no father, than a father who's never loved you?"

"You can't know that! Listen to yourself!"

"I *do* know it! I heard him say it! He hates me and he doesn't want me! He hit me!"

Connie broke off as sobs wracked her whole body. In an instant, the pressure burst into the open from the deep of her mind, spilling the emotional maelstrom she'd carried for years. Once she started, she couldn't stop, and the tears only added to her exhaustion. Before long, she just felt like an empty shell of flesh, hollowed from the inside out.

"You are cruel!" she snarled, the words like darts.

"*I'm* cruel?" Heloise barked back. "Can you even hear what *you're* saying to *me*? Didn't it cross your mind that there might be good reason, why I said no?"

"I don't care!" Connie yelled. Gulls flew from the Leap with frantic screams. "You've got eight sisters to play with and love. I've got nobody. I don't care what you have to say. Goodbye!"

87

She turned on her heel and ran away, hands covering her face dejectedly. She didn't stop until she reached her house, not even bothering to keep quiet in case she woke everyone. She snatched her drawing of Heloise off the wall, took it to the fireplace and threw it into the grate to burn. Then she buried herself in her blankets.

The last image in her mind was a memory of Heloise's face, contorted with rage and wounded pride. Connie found a shred of contentment in that, before she cried herself into slumber.

She was too exhausted to notice how the wind began blowing outside, making the sash of her window creak.

Chapter  Seven

Connie slept deeply, too fatigued to even dream. The night hours rolled off her like water over rock. But it barely felt like she'd closed her eyes before a heavy hand appeared on her shoulder and roughly shook her awake.

She moaned, squinted up at the intruder, and immediately recognised the heavy bulk of her father. As soon as he saw her eyes were open, he shoved something in her face. Connie shrunk back, still not completely lucid, and winced as stiffness registered in her limbs.

"What is this?" Albert hissed, brandishing the thing at her.

Connie blinked hard to clear her vision. Her heart leapt with nerves. He was holding the drawing which she'd tossed in the embers. It had only partially burned away, and even though an arm was missing, the tail was still very visible.

"Why did you do this?" Albert demanded again, voice harder now. "Tell me!"

"I... it's nothing, Papa," Connie said. "It's just a silly drawing I made a few days ago."

Albert looked at her for a long moment. Then he grasped her wrist, pulling her from the bed. Connie stumbled awkwardly, trying to get her aching legs to work, as he strode into the main room. He went to the window and spun her around to face him.

"You take me for a fool?" he said. "I know you've never really believed in all the legends. So why would you go ahead and draw one?"

Connie wrinkled her nose at the smell of alcohol on his breath. Behind her, rain was lashing against the glass, heavy clouds obscuring the coming sunrise. Her body felt like a leaden weight; heart thumping deeply. Her swollen cheek tingled with worry.

Albert gave an indecipherable snarl. He let go of her and grabbed his bottle, which was already half empty. He stuck the neck between his lips and gave a heavy swig before slamming it back down on the windowsill.

"Listen to me. You tell me right this minute, why you drew that! Tell me! *Now!*"

Fear raced in Connie's blood, getting the better of her. She realised there was no way he'd leave her alone until she confessed something, and she was too tired to think of an excuse. So she swallowed, and spoke the truth.

"There are mermaids. In the cove. I met one. That's a drawing of her."

Albert's eyes sparkled. "Who is she? Did she tell you her name?"

"She's called Heloise," Connie said. "She's... my half-sister, Papa."

Albert's face turned white in an instant. The silence was a shock to Connie, and she backed up against the window, unsure of what to do now. The panes were cold, trembling with the force of the weather. Albert's fingers crushed the paper in a fist.

Dawn suddenly staggered into the room, clinging onto the doorframe for support. Her hair was bedraggled and greasy, but her eyes were alert, obviously having heard the ruckus.

"Albert, what in heaven's name is going on?" she snapped.

But Albert didn't answer her, keeping his eyes firmly on Connie. He let the drawing fall to the floor, and grasped her wrist again, more frantic this time.

"Was her mother there?" he breathed. "Raniira? Was she there? Answer me!"

"Albert, stop bullying her!" Dawn cried. She forced herself between them, pushing Connie behind her protectively.

"Answer me, Connie Marner!" Albert shouted.

"Yes!" Connie wrenched herself free and held her face in her hands. "Yes, she is! I saw her singing!"

Albert's cheeks turned ruddy again. "What? Raniira has been in that cove singing for me, and you didn't tell me?"

"Stop talking about Raniira!" Dawn yelled. "For God's sake, Albert! Can't you just admit you imagined her when the ship went down? Just stop it! Right now!"

"How dare you say I imagined her!" Albert raged, thrusting his face up close. "I have a daughter by her!"

"Then why don't you go to them, huh?" Connie shoved her way from behind her mother and fixed all her fury on Albert. "I heard what you said about me the other night, and I hate you back! I hate you more than anyone in the world! You are a horrible father!"

She paused, panting. She wasn't sure how Albert would react to her outburst, and instinctively shied away in case he struck her again. But she was surprised to see his expression soften a little, and something almost like remorse fleet through his eyes. He reached his hand towards her gently, but Connie shifted her head so he couldn't touch her.

"Go on," she snarled. "Go to Raniira. I don't care."

Albert stared at her. Connie almost found herself hoping he'd hear the hurt in her words and suddenly change, like people did in the old fairytales. He'd see the error of his ways; repent to his family here on the land; become a better man, and help them survive and be happy.

But he didn't. Without another word, he turned around and grabbed his old sailing cap from the hook on the wall. Pulling it over his greying hair, he swung open the door and stalked down the path.

Dawn let out a little cry and flew after him. Connie stayed where she was, dazed, but then forced herself to walk to the doorway. Rain blew in, soaking the front of her body. Albert was on the street now, and Dawn had flung herself at his feet, arms wrapped around him as she pleaded with him to stay.

A memory of Raniira's story played in Connie's mind. This was probably exactly what the mermaid had done, eleven years ago, in an attempt to make her lover change his mind.

Connie watched as Albert shook Dawn off and moved away in the direction of the Leap, not glancing back over his shoulder at all. It was only once he'd disappeared that Connie ran to help her mother, who had collapsed piteously on the cobblestones. The two of them threw their arms

94

around each other, caught in the same open bubble of shock. Waves crashed against the quay and covered them with foamy spray.

As Dawn wept, Connie heard the mystical voice of Raniira through the howling wind. And then, singing a different tune, she heard Heloise too – accompanied by the faraway burst of thunder.

"You should be happy now," Connie whispered spitefully. "Now you've got everything I never had."

*

The rain fell steadily all the morning, and there had been a little more thunder, but Connie didn't let it bring her down. The storm was far out at sea and the edge of it had probably just fallen on Trewhella as the cloud hit the higher ground. She knew from experience that it would blow over by the end of the day.

In fact, the weather was the last thing on her mind. True to her suspicions, Albert hadn't returned. She'd put her mother to bed with some more tea and mussel broth, and would have stayed with her were it not for the amount of work she needed to do. Before tiredness could get the better of her again, Connie made her way through the mound of laundry, hanging it over a frame near the fireplace to dry. As she waited for more water to heat up for the basin, she cleaned the house and set about preparing dinner.

Florence had been no help at all; she'd taken herself to her usual chair and sat clutching her flask, rocking back and forth agitatedly. Knowing she wasn't faking it, Connie tucked her in a blanket and returned to the chores. She kept going to check on both Florence and Dawn whenever she found a spare moment, but didn't get much response out of either of them. It bleakly occurred to her that nothing had changed after all.

Close to midday, the temperature dropped, so Connie pulled on a shawl. It felt strange after the summer mugginess, and she wished it wasn't raining so she could go outside for some air. But then she was startled by an ear-piercing shriek from Florence.

"Granny!" she cried, running into the back. "What's the matter?"

"It's unnatural!" Florence cried, gesturing wildly at the window. "Don't you hear it? The song of the storm, on the wind!"

"Be quiet, Florence, please!" Dawn called from the next room.

"Connie!" Florence snatched at the girl, eyes wide. "Lass... can't you hear her? You must be able to hear her! She's offended! She's bringing a maelstrom!"

Connie glanced outside, watching the rain streaking down the glass. "Granny, please! I need to go and do the work."

She gently pried Florence's fingers away from her arm and slipped back into the main room, leaning against the door to get her breath. The wind blew down the chimney and flared the embers, spraying ash across the floor. Groaning, Connie grabbed the dustpan and brush, swept it up and opened the window a crack to tip it outside. Rain exploded in her face and she slammed the shutters closed.

She smoothed her apron wearingly; then crossed to her mother's room. Dawn seemed smaller than ever in the bed she'd shared with Albert, coughing into a handkerchief. Connie had managed to warm her up when they'd returned to the house, dressing her in layers and towelling her hair dry before taking her to rest. But now the fatigue and illness was really showing on her face, and all they could do was wait for the fever to break.

"How are you feeling, Mama?" Connie asked in a small voice.

Dawn heaved a sigh. "I'll live." She raised an arm. "Come here, darling."

Connie obeyed, perching on the edge of the mattress. Dawn stroked her cheek tenderly, being careful not to press too hard. As Connie had thought, the bruise had come through, and her flesh was now swollen and dark.

"Does that hurt?" Dawn asked.

Connie shook her head. "Not really."

"I'm sorry I didn't hear it."

"It's not your fault."

"Yes it is. I never thought he'd snap like that. And if he did, I'd have wanted it to be at me any day, rather than you." Dawn wiped some tears away. "Connie, you know you shouldn't have shouted back, don't you? He's your father. His word is law."

"Is that why you stayed with him, Mama?" Connie nibbled her lips tensely.

Dawn took hold of her daughter's hand and squeezed it. "I stayed with him because I loved him."

"Why?" Connie couldn't keep the confusion out of her voice. "How could you?"

"Because I remember the man I fell in love with. Back when we were both young and courting. He was a different man. A better man," Dawn replied wistfully. She coughed hard, doubling over, and Connie waited until she had finished before offering her tea. Dawn took it with a grateful nod.

"A big part of your father did go down with the *Senara*, dear," she carried on. "If it hadn't been for that, we would have had the perfect family. Don't you think for a minute that he did not love you."

"But I heard him say it," Connie insisted. "He said he didn't want me."

"I've known him for a lot longer than you have," said Dawn, "and I know that was the booze talking. Gin does strange things to a man's mind. You must have seen the sailormen always staggering around like your father did, every single time they went to the tavern after docking.

"He's done some terrible things, yes. But I can't bring myself to hate him for them, because he still came back to be with us. You must believe me. He *did* love you, and I love you too, my dear little Connie. I should tell you that more often. You are my golden girl."

Connie's heart swelled; and she lowered herself onto her mother's breast, hugging her as tightly as she dared. Her tears soaked into the blanket, and she let them come, unashamed. Dawn put her arms over Connie's shoulders and ran her fingers through her hair.

"What happened to your ribbon?"

Connie swallowed. "I lost it." She looked up. "Do you want me to fetch you a spoonful of honey, to soothe your throat?"

In response, Dawn coughed again, and nodded. Connie smiled; then went back into the front room to find the jar.

Chapter  Eight

The gale intensified as afternoon drew in, howling through the streets. The sound reminded Connie of the old saying, that when it blew like this, it was full of the final cries of the weeping widows. Florence's shrieks grew louder too, and Dawn had long since given up telling her to settle.

Connie tied her hair back with a shred of string, and folded the dry laundry. She went to throw the next load into the basin, when she heard hysterical shouting from outside. Shocked, she looked out of the window, squinting through the rain, and saw a crowd gathering above the quay.

Alarm shot through her. Nobody in their right mind would go out in this weather, unless something was very wrong.

"Mama, Granny, stay here!" she called over her shoulder, before darting through the door. She wrestled it shut behind her and ran as fast as she could down the path, puddles splashing over her legs. She covered her hair with her shawl, but it wasn't long before she was soaked to the skin.

"What's going on?" she yelled when she reached the throng. "What's happened?"

It was impossible to be heard over the frantic cries and shrieking wind, but Connie's answer came as soon as she looked up. Between the high harbour walls, the sea was raging, sending huge waves crashing into the stone. The ships were swaying crazily, tugging at their moorings, and some smaller boats had broken free. The quay was already submerged, and the water rising rapidly, surging towards the village.

But that wasn't what everyone was pointing at. Outside the breakwaters, Connie could see the fishing ship that had set out a few days before, run aground near the cove beneath the Lover's Leap.

"Alright, quiet down, you lot!" bellowed one of the old seamen, standing on a crate so he could be seen. "Listen! I want every able-bodied lad with me! We need to help them before they all go under! Everyone, get to higher ground at the farms! There's no waiting out this deluge now!"

His words threw instant sense into the crowd, and everyone scattered. Connie was shoved back and forth in the ruckus, struggling to stay on her feet. As men ran forward to ready a rescue, she returned to the house, lightning forking brightly overhead.

"Mama! Granny, come on, we need to go to the farms! The streets are flooding!" she screamed, bursting into Dawn's room. Before her mother could say a word, Connie pulled her up and forced a pair of boots onto her feet.

"What did I tell you?" Florence wailed, coming to the doorway. She looked at Connie and cackled madly. "Oh, disrespect! She's angry, oh so angry!"

Connie worked as quickly as she could to get everyone ready. When she ran out of shawls, she raided the laundry pile, desperate to make sure

Dawn and Florence would be as protected as possible. Dawn tucked her coin purse into her dress, and Connie ran to her room for her teddy.

She was about to leave when her eye caught the speckled conch shell on her nightstand. Barely thinking, she snatched that too, before leading the way back into the storm.

The clouds were so thick; they had completely blotted out the sun, and made everything seem like evening. Only the lightning, which now came every few seconds, lit the streets enough to remind everyone it was still afternoon. Each bolt was immediately followed by a crash of thunder, directly overhead, with such power that it shook the earth.

Connie hurriedly joined the exodus of others running for shelter in the farms above the village. Everyone was desperate to keep away from the raging water, in case lightning hit the waves. A lot of people fell on the slippery cobbles, including Dawn, but Connie pulled her back onto her feet before she could hurt herself. Florence went on ahead, waving her arms, still shrieking.

After what felt like an age, they made it to the top, and hurried inside the hay barns. The farmers were already there, helping people get settled. It wasn't the first time the villagers had been evacuated like this in a storm, but it was the first that Connie had taken part in. She was relieved when two farmhands came forward to help her with Florence and Dawn, and she collapsed onto her knees, shaking with adrenaline.

"Mermaids!" Florence cried from somewhere near the back, where it was warmer.

Connie heard the wind change direction. Listening through the howls of it blowing over rooftops and around corners, she thought she could hear a single voice. Concentrating hard, she recognised it with a jolt.

"Heloise," she breathed, looking at the shell still clasped in her hand. She pressed it to her ear, and sure enough, heard the sea echoing from inside: as full of fury and power as the weather.

Connie remembered the final expression on her sister's face, which had given her so much spiteful joy to see. Now, it sent a jolt of sick horror through her. Heloise's pride ran deep; Connie had seen that from the first. She'd played on it, and now like any scorned mermaid, Heloise had repaid the disrespect by singing up a storm.

Her decision was made in an instant. Leaving her teddy behind, Connie snatched the conch and fled back out into the tempest. Thunder rolled above her, but she swallowed her fear as she ran away from Trewhella.

She knew it would be suicide to attempt reaching the cove, so she went for the next best place, struggling up the Lover's Leap. She fought to keep her footing on the wet grass, wiping rain and tears out of her eyes. Her fingers went numb around the shell.

At the summit, she looked down on a seething grey sea, completely unlike the blue tranquil body she'd so often seen. The cove was practically invisible beneath the water; the rocks nowhere to be seen and giant waves spewing up the side of the Leap. Further out, the ship had broken in two, rigging torn free of its bonds. The secondary boat was already there, tethered to the stern, helping the crew get to safety.

"Heloise!" Connie screamed into the storm. "Please stop this!"

The wind ripped her words away. She struggled to breathe as the air churned, sending her hair into a frenzy. Below, the rescue boat began to make its way back to the harbour.

"I know you can hear me!" Connie yelled; her chest straining. "Heloise, I'm sorry! Please! I didn't mean what I said! *Heloise!*"

The stress broke something inside her and she felt her nose start to bleed again. She wiped it on her shawl, hanging onto the shell with her other hand. And then she heard her sister's voice spinning around her, chillingly beautiful.

"No more gales or heavy weather.

One more day!

Only one more day together.

Only one more day!"

Before Connie could do anything more, the wind suddenly intensified, knocking her off balance. She cried out, backpedalling, but crashed down and rolled off the front of the Leap.

Her scream was lost in the gale as she saw the rocks coming up to meet her. She screwed her eyes closed, waiting for the impact; then heard a loud crash as a wave slammed into the cliff, high above the cove. She plunged into the water, and was dragged out into the open.

Numbly amazed to be unhurt, she opened her eyes, struggling to see amid the debris churned from the seabed. Kicking frantically, she made for the surface, but the fall had disorientated her, and she wasn't sure of her direction. Another wave ploughed into her, pushing her back towards the Leap. She narrowly missed slamming against its face, but then noticed the toothy rocks that formed the edge of the cove.

She grabbed hold of one, and the water fell away around her. Connie gulped oxygen, pressing herself against the rock like a lifeline. However, it quickly turned out to be a death trap.

The waves shot over her again, pressing her down on her back. Barnacles scraped her shoulders and bubbles streamed out of her nose. She clamped a hand over her face to stop them, fighting to get up, but the currents were too strong, churning between the rocks, and the water never dropped low enough to help her.

She stared at the surface in panic. She was going to drown. She would follow the *Senara* widows, taking the blow for her father one last time.

She turned her head to the open sea, and thought she saw a lone figure in the water, silhouetted by a lightning flash. It had the body of a girl, and the tail of a dolphin, and was simply hanging there, as though contemplating whether to leave her.

Connie lost all strength and let the last of her oxygen free. As the sea flooded her lungs, she let her eyes close, imagining a hand curling around her arm. She felt herself floating, with the water flying past her with unbelievable speed. Sand appeared under her back before she lost consciousness.

Chapter  Nine

It seemed as though she'd been lying inside herself for years, slowly making the ascent away from life. The weight of the water inside her felt somewhere far away; it didn't even bother her that salt was stinging her nose.

Then a different pressure appeared on her chest, pushing vigorously in a continuous motion. That was uncomfortable. Connie tried to roll away from it, but her body was heavy and unresponsive. Then someone blew air down her throat and continued the compressions. Just as Connie had a mind to shout at whoever it was to leave her alone, water shot through her and spurted out over her face.

She coughed violently, clutching at her stomach and head. Every part of her body hurt. Her legs were trembling with cramps; pins and needles were forming in her hands. But when she opened her eyes, she was astonished to find she'd somehow managed to keep hold of the conch, and it was undamaged.

She blinked hard, looking around. Sitting beside her, wet hair plastered to her face, was Heloise.

For a moment, neither of them said anything, and just stared at each other. Heloise's lips were pressed tightly together, eyes wide with anxiety. The starfish had crawled off her head and settled on the side of her neck. Trailing over her shoulder, Connie could see one of the ends of the pink ribbon, still tied into the mermaid's hair.

"Are you alright?" Heloise asked.

Connie nodded; one hand still on her chest. "Did you do that? Save me?"

"Yes. I did what my mother did, when she saved our father. The kiss of life."

Connie's breathing shuddered as she sat up properly, glancing at the surroundings. They were in a small inlet which she recognised as being on the other side of the Leap. Trewhella was nowhere to be seen, but she could tell the gradient of this beach was higher, because the crashing waves still left a small strip of dry sand. Behind them, there was a wonky trail leading from the sea, where Heloise had dragged her to safety.

Connie's shawls fell off her shoulders, but she didn't bother with them, and instead just swiped her hair away from her mouth. Her words tangled around her tongue.

"I'm so sorry," she said. "I didn't mean to be so cruel to you. I never should have said all that; it wasn't your fault."

Heloise smirked, tilting her head. "I suffer from the mermaid's malady too easily: too much pride," she replied. "Listen, you must believe me, I didn't sing this up to hurt you. I never wanted to hurt anybody, I swear. I was just angry, and I've never brought on a storm before. I didn't know it would be so powerful. I never meant for this to happen."

"I do believe you," said Connie, holding out her arms.

The two of them embraced, holding each other tightly as the thunder continued to roar overhead. Tears spilled from Connie's eyes, and she hid her face in Heloise's hair, breathing in the rich briny scent on her cold skin.

"Hey!" Connie cried, pointing over Heloise's shoulder.

Sitting on a rock near the Leap was Raniira, her tail just skimming the waves. At her side, Albert was sitting, an arm curled fondly around her waist. He looked the happiest Connie had ever seen him. There was a renewed shine in his eyes, and a smile highlighted his lips as he surveyed his daughters together for the first time.

"My sisters are here!" said Heloise.

Connie followed her gaze and noticed eight other figures in the water, looking into the inlet with interest. They were all older, ranging from about eighteen to thirty, and while they shared the distinctive sleek skin, there were marked differences in them that set them apart from Heloise. Some had dark or shorter hair; others seemed taller than their siblings. But Connie could tell they were all of the same family, and she heard their voices on the wind like an ethereal choir.

"The storm must have caught their attention," Heloise muttered. "They are stronger than me. They'll be able to suppress it quicker."

"Is that what they're doing now?"

"Yes."

Connie glanced one more time at Raniira and Albert. The mermaid had slipped into the water now – notably calmer already – and was coaxing her lover down to join her. Albert willingly followed until he was beside her, and the two shared a passionate kiss.

Then he looked back at Connie, met her eyes evenly, and gave her a sincere nod. It was a simple gesture, but in it, Connie saw the apology she'd longed for, as well as all the love her mother had spoken of.

Truly moved, and full of understanding, she returned the gesture. Albert smiled, before he grasped Raniira, and they both dived under the waves.

Connie sniffled, wiping away tears. Her nose had stopped bleeding, and even her bruise felt as though it had healed a little.

"Heloise," she whispered, "thank you for not leaving me there, in the rocks."

"I never would have," her sister assured. "I told you."

"No, you didn't," Connie frowned. You said you wouldn't let me come away with you."

"Why do you think I said that?" said Heloise. "Every single one of my mother's loves has drowned when they join her in our home. Our father will soon follow. But I am not my mother. And even though I love you, I'd never take you where we couldn't be together. At least this way, in different worlds, we still can be." She hesitated. "Can't we?"

"Of course," replied Connie surely. "I would never be without you."

*

By the time Connie finally returned to Trewhella, the storm had blown itself out, and the mermaid voices vanished with the wind. The quayside was devastated, but she saw the rescue boat coming through the gap in the breakwaters, full of survivors from the wrecked ship. Connie could tell even from where she stood, most of the crew had been saved. Relief bloomed in her chest that at least this time, there would be no repeat of the *Senara*.

She made her way inside the barn, edging past the farmer, who was going around offering cups of soup. She found Dawn almost immediately, lying on some hay and fanning her face with her hand. Her mother was still clammy and coughing, and Connie flew to her side.

"Mama, how are you?" she asked worriedly.

"Why are you soaking wet?" Dawn gasped. "You didn't go out in that, did you?"

"Erm... yes, I did."

"You silly child! What did I tell you, not to go off again? You could have been swept off the cliff!"

Connie bit her tongue, quickly changing the subject. "The village is in a bad way. I think we'll be here for a while yet."

"They've mentioned we'll stay the night, and people might start heading back tomorrow if the waters have gone down," Dawn replied. "Oh... what are we going to do? The laundry will be destroyed, I'll have no job. We need to get some money..."

"Don't worry about that, Mrs Marner," the farmer suddenly said from beside them. "I've been meaning to find a milkmaid to help me with some new cows I've got coming next week. Would you be up for that?"

Dawn's eyes shone in relief. "Oh, sir... that would be wonderful. I don't know how to thank you!"

"You don't need to thank me, just get yourself better," returned the farmer. "Now have some soup. You drink some too, lass. We don't want you getting poorly as well."

Connie gratefully took two of the cups from his tray. He winked at her; then moved away to see to the people near the back of the barn. Connie handed a soup to her mother before taking a sip of her own.

The milkmaid offer had given renewed vigour to Dawn already, and Connie was now sure she would pull through the illness. Perceptions were different up on the farms because none of the *Senara*'s crew had been from north of the main village. Among the farmers, the Marners were simply unfortunates who had been dealt a bad lot. There would be no hardships for them now.

Connie licked her cup clean, letting the soup work its warmth into her bones. By the time she'd finished, most of the excess water had drained out of her clothes, leaving them damp but not freezing. The storm had cleared the mugginess, and she took deep breaths of sweet salty air, never having been so glad for oxygen in her life.

"Where's Granny Florence?" she asked after returning their cups to the farmer.

"Outside, I think," said Dawn, handing over her daughter's teddy bear. It was muddied beyond belief, but in one piece, and Connie hugged it affectionately.

She ran to the exit, leaving the heavy smell of damp hay behind her. The cloud was dissipating when she stepped into the open, revealing a setting sun bleeding over the sea.

"Red sky at night, sailor's delight," she heard Florence muttering. She turned to see the old lady standing hunched near the path leading to the harbour. Connie approached and stood by her side.

"How are you, Granny?" she asked.

"Sailorman's delight, red sky tonight," Florence carried on, and a few passing villagers rolled their eyes. Florence quietened; then threw a wry smirk at Connie. "Came out of nowhere, didn't it?"

"It sure did."

"Don't upset mermaids."

Connie smiled to herself; then noticed how Florence was just holding her cup of soup as though she'd forgotten it was there.

"Aren't you going to drink that?" she coaxed. "It will warm you up."

"No," said Florence with absolute lucidity. "I want fillet for dinner."

Connie couldn't suppress a chuckle. She looked down, at her teddy in one hand and conch shell in the other: her dearest possessions saved from the storm. Comforted by their presence, she stood with Florence, and the two of them gazed out to the open sea.

Chapter  Ten

Cornwall, 1887

Sitting on the summit of the Lover's Leap, Connie absent-mindedly tugged blades of grass out of the ground and held them up to drift away on the wind. The moon had long since risen, and was fat and full in the sky, filling the cove below with its silvery light. The conch rested in her lap, looking exactly the same as it had on the day when she first took it home.

She glanced over her shoulder, down the slope towards Trewhella. In some ways, it was barely recognisable from her childhood. It had advanced into something much greater than its humble origins, spreading back from a newly-reconstructed quayside. The remains of the shipwreck had broken apart and washed away long ago, and now there was nothing except whispered tales to say what had happened there.

Connie could now truly understand what Florence had meant, when she'd claimed to be part of a world that was slipping into history. The old woman had passed away soon after the great storm, but like her, Connie had never left the village, and she saw it grow and change. She witnessed the wooden ships, with their romantic rigging and sails, give way to metal vessels topped with smoking funnels. Time rolled forward, slowly and surely towards the next century, sweeping Connie along in its current.

Since that summer so long ago, people became even more ignorant of the mysteries of the sea. Fishermen no longer paid heed to old wives' tales that spoke of people beneath the waves. There were many across the country who even claimed such beings could never exist. The carving in the church became nothing more than a novelty to fascinate children. Ships still went down; bad catches were made; storms would blow up out of nowhere with a haunting melody on their winds. Nobody cared to listen anymore.

But Connie did, just as she had all her life. As she inhaled the magnificent air of the coast, she thought back to this night fifty years ago, when she first heard the song. She put the shell against her ear, waiting patiently, until she saw Heloise's silhouette appear in the mouth of the cove below.

Connie smiled widely and began making her way down. She had no control over the current of time. But she would always have these beloved moments with her sister: swimming together, or just talking and laughing, until the night was gone.

ABOUT THE AUTHOR

E. C. Hibbs is an award-winning author and artist, often found lost in the woods or in her own imagination. Her writing has been featured in the British Fantasy Society Journal, and she has provided artworks in various mediums for clients across the world. She is also a calligrapher and live storyteller, with a penchant for fairytales and legends. She adores nature, fantasy, history, and anything to do with winter. She lives with her family in Cheshire, England.

Learn more and join the Batty Brigade at
www.echibbs.weebly.com

Printed in Great Britain
by Amazon

79127973R00071